A
TALE
—
SAJLSIS
OWT

Annick Press gratefully
acknowledges the support of
The Canada Council and the
Ontario Arts Council.

Canadian Cataloguing
in Publication Data

Johnson, Gillian K.
Saranohair

ISBN 1-55037-211-4

I. Title.

PS8569.O55S3 1992   jC813'.54
C91-094867-4   PZ7.J6Sa 1992

Distributed in Canada and
the USA by:
Firefly Books Ltd.,
250 Sparks Avenue
Willowdale, Ontario
M2H 2S4

Design by Pol Turgeon
The art in this book was
rendered in pen and ink. The
text has been set in
Copperplate by Zibra Inc.

Printed on recycled paper and
bound in Canada by D.W.
Friesen & Sons,
Altona, Manitoba.

TO MY MOTHER AND FATHER

IT WAS ONCE UPON A TIME NOT LONG AGO THAT THERE LIVED TWO SISTERS WHOSE NAMES WERE: O-STEFANEFANIE AND SARANOHAIR. THE TWO SISTERS DECIDED THAT THEY WOULD LIKE TO DIG A HOLE IN THE GROUND. OR RATHER, O-STEFANEFANIE THOUGHT IT MIGHT BE A PLEASANT WAY TO PASS THE DAY AND SARANOHAIR HAD NOTHING BETTER TO DO THAN WHAT HER BIGGER OLDER SISTER WANTED DONE.

FOR THE FIRST THREE HOURS THE DIGGING WAS FINE. THE SAND WAS SMOOTH, THE SUN WAS WARM AND THE SKY WAS BLUE. AND EVEN BETTER FOR O-STEFANEFANIE, SHE DIDN'T GET ONE SPOT ON HER NEW RED DRESS.

BUT AS IT OFTEN HAPPENS WHEN DIGGING HOLES, THEY HIT A ROCK. SARAHONHAIR TRIED TO PULL IT OUT BUT IN DOING SO SHE FELL INTO THE HOLE AND DISAPPEARED. AFTER A FEW MINUTES, O-STEFANEFANIE GREW WORRIED.

WHAT SHOULD O-STEFANEFANIE DO?

A SHOULD O-STEFANEFANIE RUN FOR HELP?

B SHOULD O-STEFANEFANIE START TO CRY?

C SHOULD O-STEFANEFANIE LIVE HAPPILY EVER AFTER?

D SHOULD O-STEFANEFANIE JUMP INTO THE HOLE TO RESCUE SARANOHAIR?

O.boohoo

B

O-STEFANEFANIE
STARTED
TO CRY.

A

O-STEFANEFANIE
RAN FOR
HELP.

O-YAY
a room to
myself

C

O-STEFANEFANIE
WENT HOME
AND LIVED
HAPPILY
EVER AFTER.

D

O-STEFANEFANIE
JUMPED
INTO THE HOLE
TO RESCUE
SARANOHAIR.

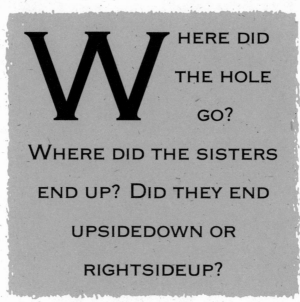

Where did the hole go? Where did the sisters end up? Did they end upsidedown or rightsideup?

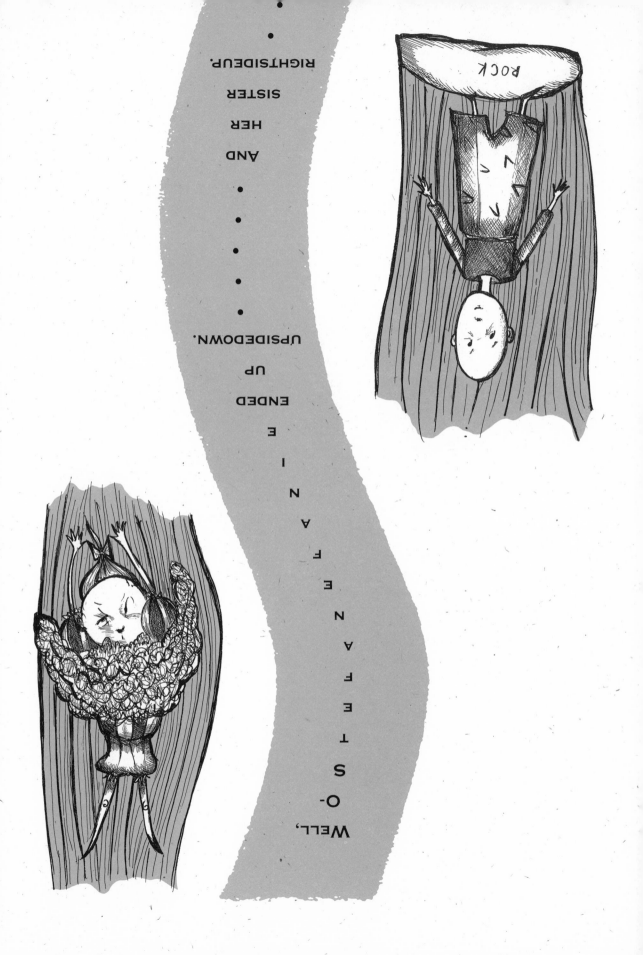

WELL, O-STEFANIE FAN ENDED UP UPSIDEDOWN. AND HER SISTER RIGHTSIDEUP.

. . .

AND

SINCE

S
A
R
A
N
O
H
A
I
R
FELL
AHEAD,
IT
WAS
ON
HER
HEAD
THAT
HER
SISTER
ENDED
UP.

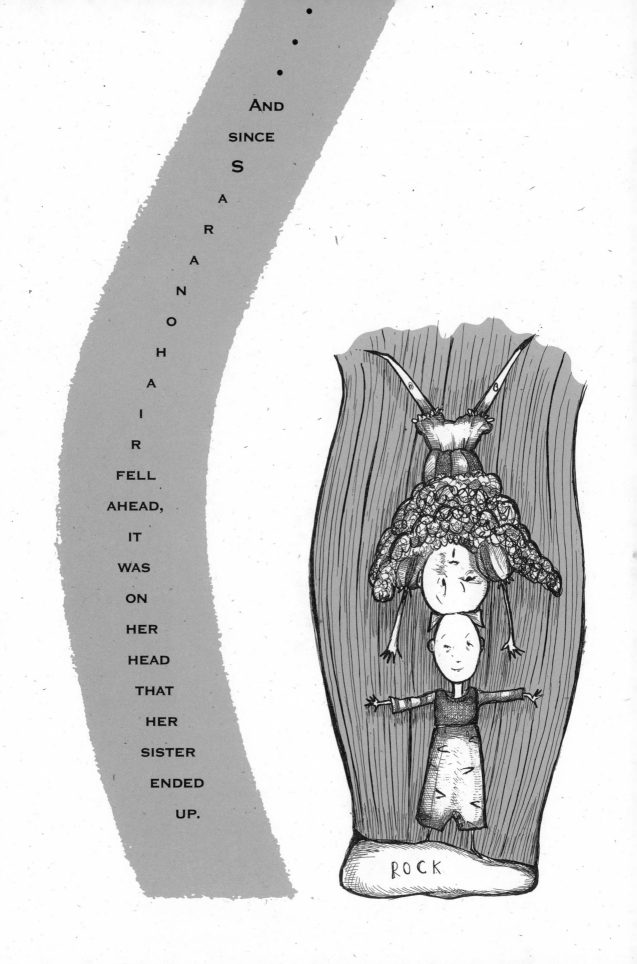

ROCK

UPSIDEDOWN

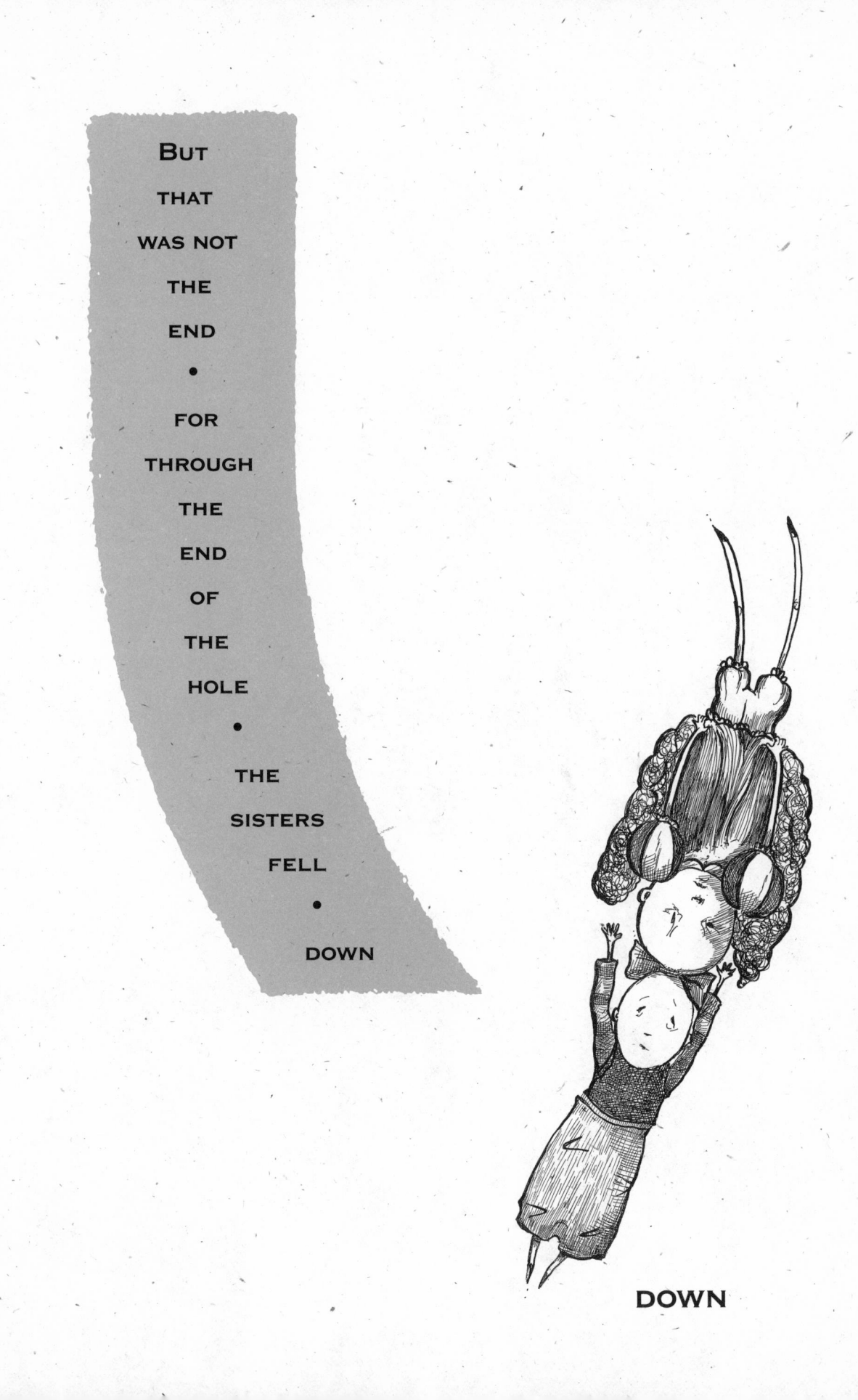

BUT

THAT

WAS NOT

THE

END

•

FOR

THROUGH

THE

END

OF

THE

HOLE

•

THE

SISTERS

FELL

•

DOWN

DOWN

DOWN

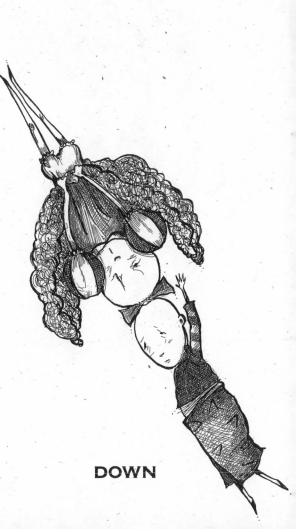

DOWN

UNTIL THEY REACHED THE GROUND, FIRST SARANOHAIR AND THEN HER SISTER TURNED UPSIDEDOWN AND PARTLY INSIDEOUT. SARANOHAIR TRIED TO STAND UP TO GET A LOOK AROUND, BUT WITH HER SISTER STUCK TO HER HEAD IT WAS HARD TO GET UP OFF THE GROUND. AND INSIDEOUT AND UPSIDEDOWN POOR O-STEFANEFANIE COULDN'T SEE A THING. ·

IF SHE HAD BEEN RIGHTSIDEUP LIKE HER SISTER,
SHE WOULD HAVE SEEN WHAT SARANOHAIR SAW,
A VERY TALL FIGURE APPROACHING FROM FAR
AWAY— A WOMAN WEARING THE STRANGEST HAT
THAT SARANOHAIR HAD EVER SEEN.

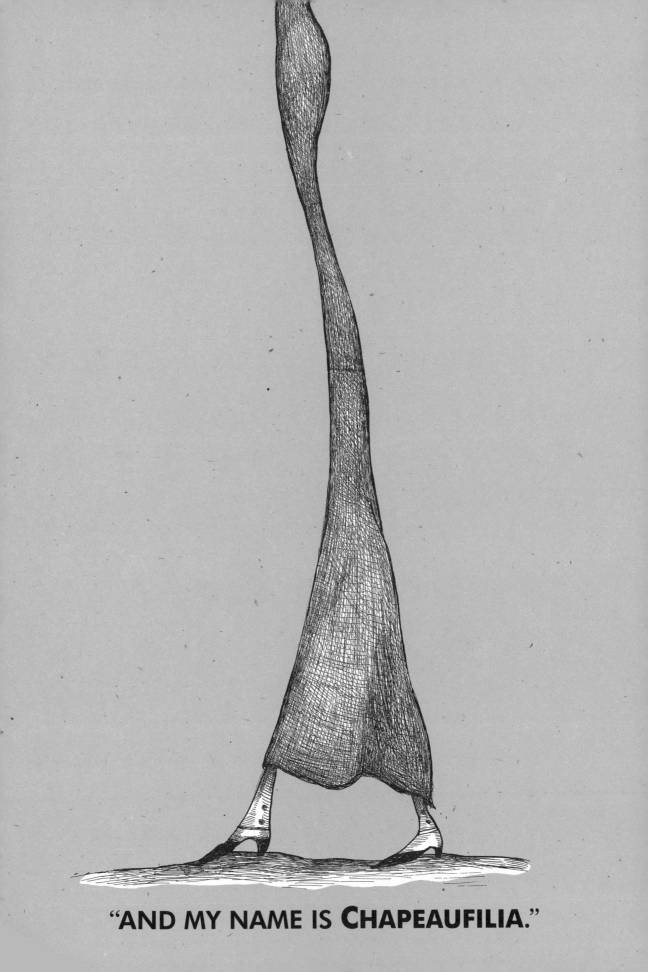

"AND MY NAME IS **CHAPEAUFILIA**."

"LOVELY, LOVELY, LOVELY," SHE CRIED,
"WHERE DID YOU GET IT?"
"WHERE DID YOU GET YOUR CHAPEAU?
WHAT A WONDERFUL HAT!"

BEFORE SARAHNAIR COULD ANSWER,
CHAPEAUFILIA TOOK HER HAND

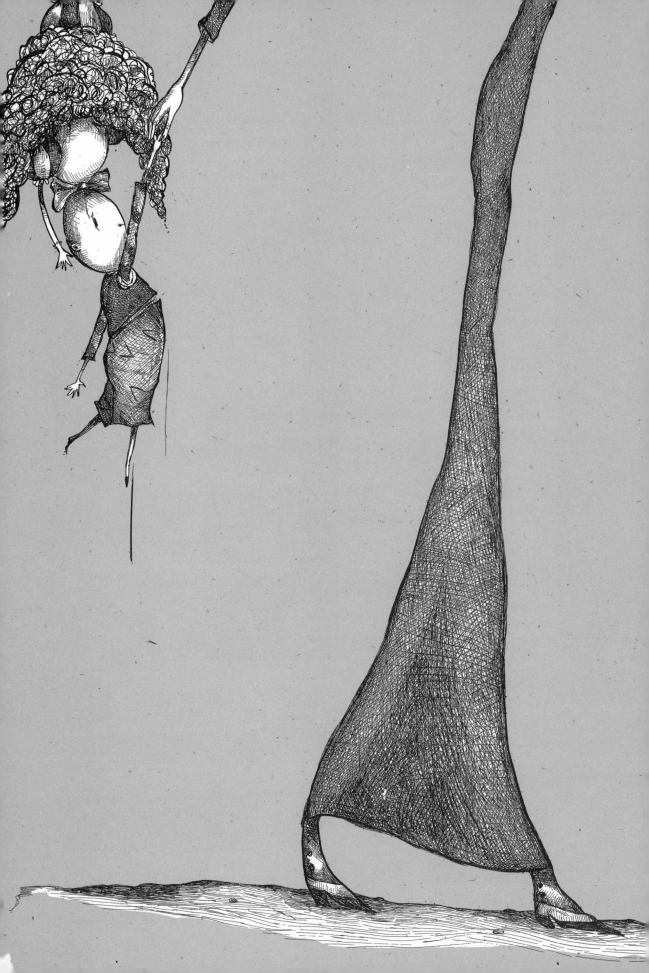

AND LED THE TWO SISTERS TO HER HAT SHOP.

CHAPEAUFILIA

PUT

SARANOHAIR AND HER

SISTER IN THE DISPLAY

WINDOW OF HER

CHAPEAU SHOP

FOR ALL THE PEOPLE

TO SEE.

AND FOR A MONTH

SHE MADE HATS

THAT LOOKED EXACTLY

LIKE

O-STEFANEFANIE

TURNED

UPSIDEDOWN

AND PARTLY INSIDEOUT.

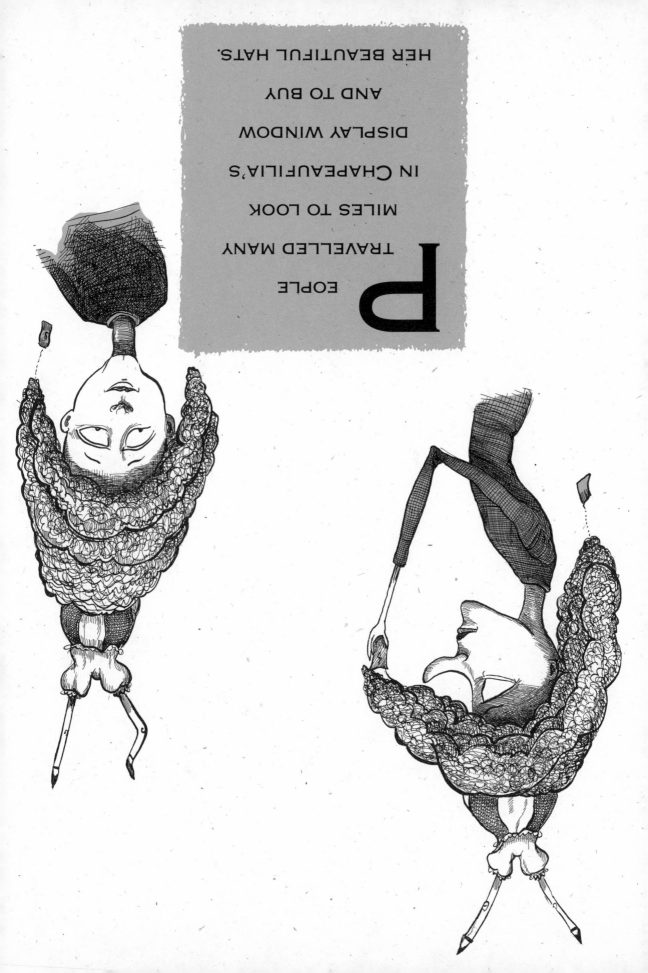

P EOPLE TRAVELLED MANY MILES TO LOOK IN CHAPEAUFILIA'S DISPLAY WINDOW AND TO BUY HER BEAUTIFUL HATS.

CHAPEAUFILIA BECAME VERY RICH.

AND SARANOHAIR BECAME VERY FAMOUS.

B

UT THEN
ONE DAY WHEN
CHAPEAUFILIA WAS
AWAY, THE INFAMOUS
MADAMA DRAT-
I-GOTTA HAVA-HAT
VISITED THE SHOP.

THE FLOOR SHOOK.

"I GOTTA HAVE THAT HAT! TAKE IT OFF! GIVE IT TO ME!" SHE DEMANDED. HER CHINS JIGGLED AS SHE SPOKE.

"BUT I CAN'T," SAID SARANOHAIR.

"WHAT!!" CRIED MADAMA DRAT I-GOTTA-HAVA-HAT.

"HOW DARE YOU DEFY ME! I'LL GO AND GET MY SCISSORS AND REMOVE IT MYSELF! I GOTTA HAVE THAT HAT!" HER ARMS JIGGLED AS SHE RUSHED OUT OF THE SHOP.

What should Saranohair do?

boo-hoo

B

SHOULD SARANOHAIR START TO CRY?

A

SHOULD SARANOHAIR DIG ANOTHER HOLE?

yipee
a chair to
myself

C

SHOULD
SARANOHAIR
TRY TO LIVE
HAPPILY
EVER
AFTER?

D

SHOULD
SARANOHAIR
RUN FOR
HELP?

to the
rescue

SARANOHAIR KNEW WHAT SHE HAD TO DO. SHE STEPPED OUT OF THE DISPLAY WINDOW AND THEN OUT OF THE BACK DOOR. SHE DIDN'T HAVE TIME TO WASTE. SHE FELL TO HER KNEES AND BEGAN TO DIG A HOLE IN THE GROUND.

SOON THE HOLE

WAS DEEP ENOUGH

TO FALL INTO.

AND SO SHE DID.

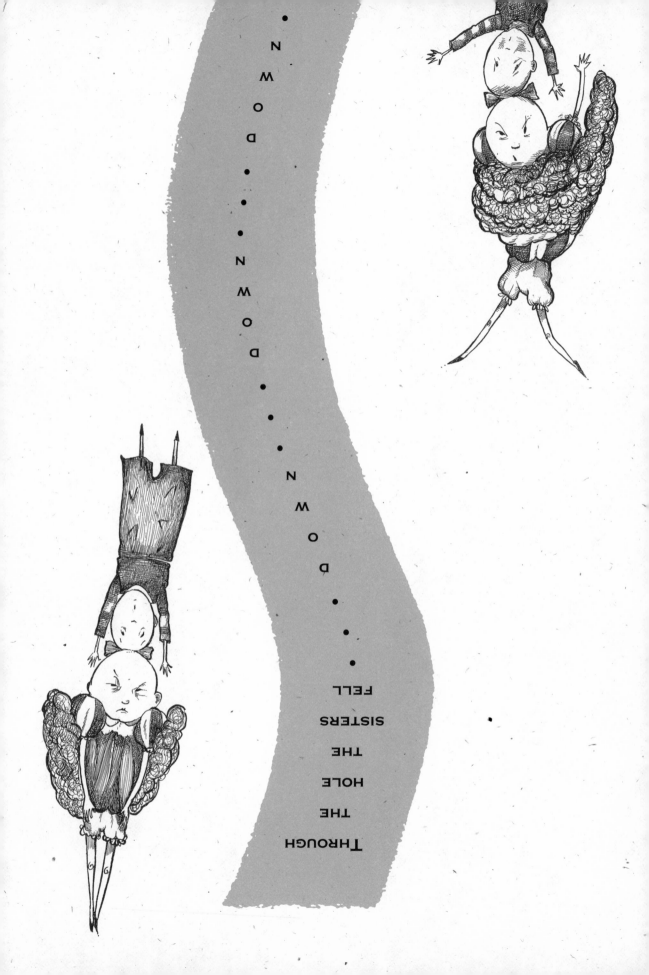

DOWN • • • • DOWN • • • DOWN • • DOWN • • •

Tʜʀᴏᴜɢʜ
THE
HOLE
THE
SISTERS
FELL

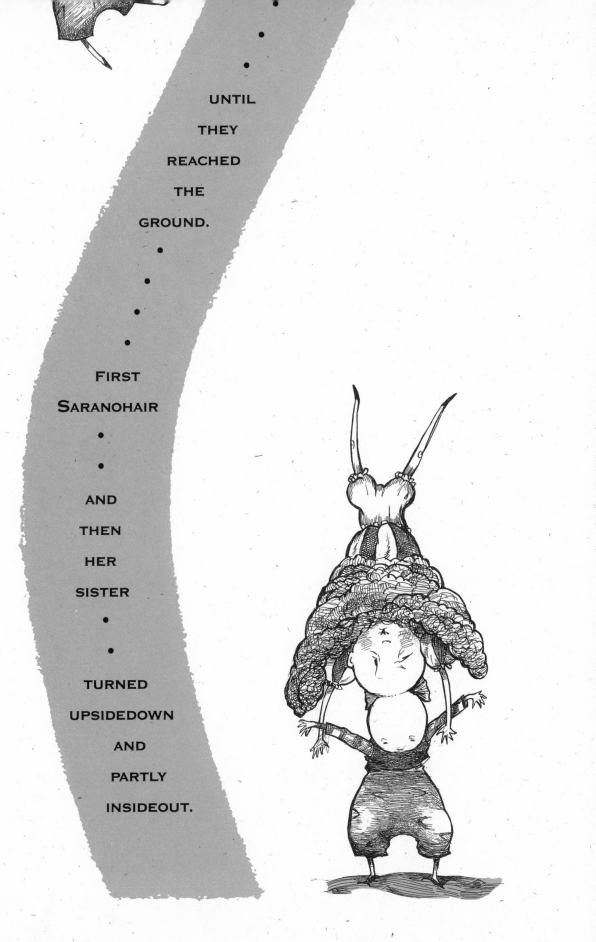

UNTIL

THEY

REACHED

THE

GROUND.

FIRST

SARANOHAIR

AND

THEN

HER

SISTER

TURNED

UPSIDEDOWN

AND

PARTLY

INSIDEOUT.

THEY WERE
BACK AT THE
BEACH.
THE SAND WAS
COOL,
THE LAKE WAS
SMOOTH
AND
THE MOON WAS
HIGH.

AND
STANDING
BEFORE THEM
WAS
THEIR FATHER,
HIS HANDS
ON HIS HIPS,
A SMILE
ON HIS FACE.
"LOVELY,
LOVELY, LOVELY!"
HE CRIED.

"WHERE DID
YOU GET IT?
WHERE DID YOU GET
YOUR CHAPEAU?
WHAT A
WONDERFUL HAT!"

"HI, DAD,"
SAID SARAHAIR.

"O, BOO-HOO,"
SAID
O-STEFANEFANIE.

"Y OU TWO LOOK
LIKE YOU'VE
HAD A ROUGH DAY,"
HE SAID.
"I CAN'T WAIT
TO HEAR
ALL ABOUT IT.
THIS TIME
I GET
THE BEDTIME STORY."